Dear Parent:

Your child's love of reading starts here!

Every child learns to read in a different way and at his or her own speed. Some go back and forth between reading levels and read favorite books again and again. Others read through each level in order. You can help your young reader improve and become more confident by encouraging his or her own interests and abilities. From books your child reads with you to the first books he or she reads alone, there are I Can Read Books for every stage of reading:

SHARED READING
Basic language, word repetition, and whimsical illustrations, ideal for sharing with your emergent reader

BEGINNING READING
Short sentences, familiar words, and simple concepts for children eager to read on their own

READING WITH HELP
Engaging stories, longer sentences, and language play for developing readers

READING ALONE
Complex plots, challenging vocabulary, and high-interest topics for the independent reader

I Can Read Books have introduced children to the joy of reading since 1957. Featuring award-winning authors and illustrators and a fabulous cast of beloved characters, I Can Read Books set the standard for beginning readers.

A lifetime of discovery begins with the magical words "I Can Read!"

Visit www.icanread.com for information
on enriching your child's reading experience.

For my always-ready-to-go-apple-picking
family, with love!
—A.S.C.

I Can Read® and I Can Read Book® are trademarks of HarperCollins Publishers.
Biscuit and the Great Fall Day
Text copyright © 2022 by Alyssa Satin Capucilli. Illustrations copyright © 2022 by Pat Schories.
All rights reserved. Printed in the United States of America.
No part of this book may be used or reproduced in any manner whatsoever without
written permission except in the case of brief quotations embodied in critical articles
and reviews. For information address HarperCollins Children's Books, a division
of HarperCollins Publishers, 195 Broadway, New York, NY 10007.
www.icanread.com

Library of Congress Control Number: 2022930515
ISBN 978-0-06-291004-2 (trade bdg.)—ISBN 978-0-06-291003-5 (pbk.)

Book design by Chrisila Maida
22 23 24 25 26 LSCC 10 9 8 7 6 5 4 3 2 1 ❖ First Edition

Biscuit
and the
Great Fall Day

story by ALYSSA SATIN CAPUCILLI
pictures by ROSE MARY BERLIN
in the style of PAT SCHORIES

HARPER
An Imprint of HarperCollinsPublishers

It's a great fall day,
Biscuit.
Woof, woof!

It's a great day to pick apples!
We have our basket, Biscuit.

8

Woof, woof!

Our friends are here

to help, too!

Woof, woof!

No jumping in the leaves now,
Biscuit.

We need lots of apples
to fill our basket.
Woof, woof!

See, Biscuit?

We can pick red apples
and green apples.

Woof, woof!

You found yellow apples, too.

This way, Biscuit.

There are more apples

over here.

Woof!

Funny puppy!

What did you find?

Woof, woof!

You found a caterpillar.

You found a squirrel, too.

Come along, Biscuit.
We still need more apples
to fill our basket.

Chee-chee!

Woof!

Chee-chee!

Woof!

Chee-chee!

Woof, woof!

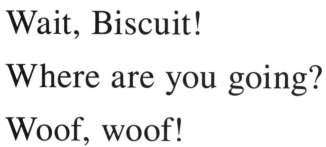

Wait, Biscuit!

Where are you going?

Woof, woof!

It's not time for
the corn maze!

Biscuit!

Where are you?

Woof! Woof! Woof! Woof!

Oh no, Biscuit.

Not the basket!

Woof!

Silly puppy!

This way now, Biscuit.
We picked lots of apples.
We can make apple pie
and applesauce.

We can go on a hayride, too!

Woof, woof!

It's been a great fall day,
Biscuit.

Woof, woof!

And the very best part
is being with you!
Woof!